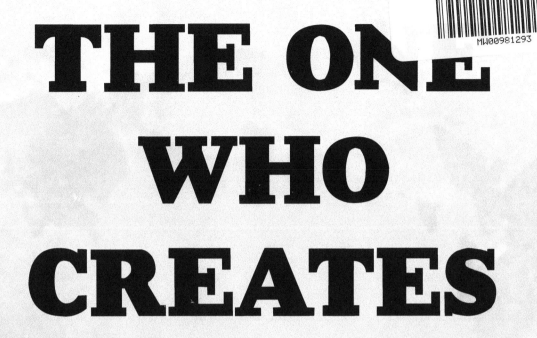

THE ONE WHO CREATES

Written by Nate Smith

Illustrated by Lydia J. Underwood

THE ONE WHO SERIES

Book 1: *The One Who Creates*
Book 2: *The One Who Hears* (Coming Soon)

WestBow Press books may be ordered through booksellers or by contacting:

WestBow Press
A Division of Thomas Nelson & Zondervan
1663 Liberty Drive
Bloomington, IN 47403
www.westbowpress.com
844-714-3454

Interior Image Credit: Lydia J. Underwood

ISBN: 978-1-6642-7094-7 (sc)
ISBN: 978-1-6642-7095-4 (e)

Library of Congress Control Number: 2022912335

Print information available on the last page.

WestBow Press rev. date: 07/20/2022

WESTBOW
PRESS®
A DIVISION OF THOMAS NELSON
& ZONDERVAN

For the creatives – both young and old

"The discipline of creation, be it to paint, compose,
write, is an effort towards wholeness."
— Madeleine L'Engle, <u>Walking on Water: Reflections on Faith and Art</u>

Introduction

On Easter weekend in 2019, I took a silent retreat at the Abbey of Gethsemani near Bardstown, Kentucky. I had planned to pray, read Scripture, and journal, as I had always done on prior retreats. But this trip felt different. Late in the first evening, I pulled up a chair to a wooden desk, lit by a lamp overhead and nestled by a twin sized bed. The blank pages of my journal stared at me as I waited on the Lord. He gently whispered to me about the next generation. Not a generation rising up, but a generation with an abundance of gifts ready to be discipled in.

Over the next three evenings, the first drafts of several children's books were written. A series simply named "The Ones Who...". Each book in the series completes its title with a specific spiritual gifting. Each book tells the story of a fictional child learning how to use their gift alongside an adult who guides them. Each book highlights the uniqueness of the gift and how to steward it. Some gifts may be considered more supernatural than others, but the greatest emphasis is on how the Gospel can be shared through the use of each one.

As you read this book, whether young or old in age, my prayer is that you will be encouraged in your own spiritual gifting, and that you will boldly follow God's lead as you use it.

In the Kentucky foothills, down in a holler, there lived a young lady named Eden Mae. She was fearless in her adventure, curious in her thoughts and, soon, unbeknownst to her, she would learn how to be a creator.

Eden Mae lived tucked away underneath the oak, hickory, beech, and sugar maple trees. She and her extended family of thirty-three were spread out among five simple log cabins. She had aunts, uncles, cousins, and animals to play with. And countless acres of creation to explore.

Her Papaw and Mamaw proudly lived in the center of them all. From the outside looking in, it might seem overwhelming for so many in close quarters. But within moments, a visitor would see that the whole family quite enjoyed one another's company.

If anyone moved, it was only to the next holler over. And they always made sure to return every Sunday for family dinner. Everyone came no matter how busy their lives were. Not even an untimely change in Appalachian weather could keep them apart. Mamaw made fried green tomatoes with the fresh produce grown from the garden. Aunt Sue cooked the greens. Cousin Bethann brought the sweet tea. Uncle Bobby baked homemade bread. And Poor Sally the pig didn't get a plea pardon.

Dessert was always apple pie topped with vanilla ice cream. Eden Mae learned early on to dig in quickly, because no one in the family ate like they were shy. Every feast was completed by Papaw sharing old family stories, and even amongst so many people, Eden Mae always felt loved and affirmed by everyone.

On weekday afternoons, Eden Mae always wandered to the same destination. She journeyed up the holler to a small log cabin, a walk that timed exactly ten minutes.

"Eden Mae," a woman would sing in a melodic tune. There at the top of the hill would be Aunt Vera with her long, black hair ushering Eden Mae to come in.

It was an inviting home with paints, books, and plants to stir Eden's curious heart. The two loved to dance to their own melodies. They giggled while exchanging made up stories. Aunt Vera always took the time to share Bible stories about designers and artists, the ones who wood-worked, crafted, and colored different garments. Over time, the two hearts began to yearn to do something of the same, yet of their own, as worship to their Creator.

One day, Aunt Vera put on an apron and rolled up her sleeves. She pulled Eden Mae in close to tell her about their new afternoon activity.

"I have blank, white scarves hidden in the cupboard. Wouldn't it be fun if we gave them some color?

Eden Mae, let's run through the hills to get the ingredients we need to turn these plain scarves into something radiant!"

The two dashed outside, neither one with socks or shoes. The dirt and rocks didn't slow them down as they raced through the trees. They collected berries, carrots, clumps of dirt, and anything their baskets could hold. Flowers, grass, and fallen leaves. With all of nature at their fingertips, they let their imaginations dream.

When their baskets were full, they ran back to sort out what they had gathered on Aunt Vera's lawn. Eden Mae then filled barrels with water, in which Aunt Vera submerged the individual ingredients.

Aunt Vera knelt and pulled in her sister's daughter, as they waited and watched new colors appear in the clear water. Both tiny and old hands then dipped sections of the white scarves into the dye. As many would, Eden Mae was eager to keep dunking the scarves from barrel to barrel. Aunt Vera led her niece to take a deep breath, as she learned how to be patient for the colors to deepen and intensify. It took the whole day to gather the ingredients and dip the scarves. And now, the whole evening for the scarves to dry.

While they waited, Eden Mae needed to learn what all the different colors symbolized.

"Colors have a purpose, especially in Heaven," said Aunt Vera. "Purple means royalty, like in Proverbs 31:22. Blue reminds our hearts to be at ease. Red is often redemption. The blood from the cross is our forever gift from Heaven. Green can mean life or it can mean greed. It is always important to ask Jesus about the colors we see. He will guide us to understand the deeper meanings of what we created. And it will always point us back to our need for a Savior."

Eden Mae headed back home as the sun began to set. She reminisced how creativity is a learning process. She thought of honest Aunt Vera, who had more to learn from trusted friends and the Spirit. Eden Mae skipped home, grateful, and excited about the process.

The following morning at half past nine, Eden Mae ran back up the holler to see the scarves swaying on Aunt Vera's clothesline. Yellow! Indigo! Magenta! Ocean Blue! With different shades of green! Each color made Eden Mae's heart full, as she giggled with glee.

With a scarf in each hand, Eden Mae danced as if to a marching band. Twirling, laughing, and singing new songs of praise. Aunt Vera and Eden Mae thanked God over and over again for being such a fun Creator. Her cousins joined in as they worshiped together.

Aunt Vera taught Eden Mae the simple craft of dying prayer scarves. Now, Eden Mae will pray and sing about what the colors mean. Songs of redemption, of love, and of peace. A simple creative lesson from Aunt Vera became a new journey of prayer and worship for her niece.

Creating will take time and commands patience in the waiting, but the end result can be both illuminating and activating. Art stirs both old and young to wonder and dream. It is also a lesson in expressing our hearts to the Creator. And an expressive way to share our spiritual journey with one another.

On Creativity

I encourage you to dive into the Biblical stories about creativity.
May these stories inspire you to dive deeper into the creative
heart within you or to learn how to encourage others.

Genesis 1 - The Creation story

Exodus 31:1-11 - God calls Bezalel by name to build His tabernacle.

2 Chronicles 1-6:11 - Solomon gathers skilled artists
and designers to build the temple again.

Matthew 13:54-55 - Jesus is known as a carpenter
before beginning his ministry.

Acts 16:13-15 - Story of Lydia, a dealer of cloth.

Acknowledgments

Thank you to the Abbey of Gethsemani for taking in visitors and providing a space for people to meet with Jesus. Thank you to Lydia for providing such beautiful illustrations and making this book come alive. Thank you to everyone who has helped me edit this book over and over again. Thank you to everyone who has listened to me talk about writing, encouraged me, and watched it come to fruition.

Father, Son, and Holy Spirit, thank you. You are the Creator and have built a creative heart within me. May my creativity honor You.

Every good and perfect gift is from above, coming down from the Father of the heavenly lights, who does not change like shifting shadows. James 1:17 ESV

CPSIA information can be obtained
at www.ICGtesting.com
Printed in the USA
LVHW072208300722
724798LV00033B/965

9 781664 270947